PHOBIA

Don't Look Down

A TALE OF TERROR BY BRANDON TERRELL
ILLUSTRATED BY MARIANO EPELBAUM

raintree

a Capstone company — publishers for children

Raintree is an imprint of Capstone Global Library Limited,
a company incorporated in England and Wales having its
registered office at 264 Banbury Road, Oxford, OX2 7DY –
Registered company number: 6695582

www.raintree.co.uk
myorders@raintree.co.uk

Original illustrations © Capstone Global Library Limited 2019
Originated by Capstone Global Library Ltd
Printed and bound in India

ISBN 978 1 4747 7174 0
23 22 2
10 9 8

British
A full c
Dritish

Everybody loves a scary story. Now you can enjoy tales that come with a good dose of fright, lots of suspense and a bit of humour too! Phobia books are about all your favourite spooky subjects such as monster aliens, haunted houses, scary dolls and magical powers that go haywire.

Read on if you dare!

ACROPHOBIA

THE FEAR OF HIGH PLACES

EVERYONE IS AFRAID
OF SOMETHING.

You may be afraid of a number of things. But a **PHOBIA** is a very special fear. It is deep and strong and long lasting. It is hard to explain why people have phobias — they just do.

Travelling by plane terrifies many people. Flying through clouds, bumping into air currents, looking down on mountaintops! Simone is not alone in her fears. Anyone who is afraid of heights would understand her reluctance to get on the Ferris wheel.

But something weird is going on at the Forever Fun Carnival. It's not just the scary rides. There's more than one fear haunting these pages...

1

I squeezed my eyes shut and balled my hands into fists. For the hundredth time in the last five minutes, I prayed the plane wouldn't crash. Which was slightly ridiculous, considering I hadn't even boarded it yet.

"Simone? Are you sure you're all right?" my mum asked. She stood behind me as I looked out of the airport's giant window at the plane I was about to take across the country.

I'd been excited about my summer trip to Grandma's for months. And it wasn't like I'd never been on a plane before. I had, lots of times.

Only this time I was flying by myself. So I pulled myself together, nodded, and said, "Perfect. Just sad to leave you." I turned to face my parents.

My mum, a worrier like me, was wringing her hands. My dad, much more relaxed, had his hands in his pockets.

"I mean, what will you both do without me?" I asked.

Dad chuckled. "Have a clean house?" he said.

I rolled my eyes.

A voice came over the speaker. "Now boarding flight 815, non-stop from Chicago to Bangor, Maine."

"All right," I said. "Here I go."

Mum and Dad gave me extra-long hugs. "Make sure you listen to the flight attendants," Mum told me. "And Grandma will be at the gate waiting for you. OK?"

"OK."

I wheeled my purple carry-on luggage to the desk and handed the man my boarding pass. "Simone Yang," he said, reading the ticket. "Flying solo, I see."

I glanced at my waving parents. "Yep."

"Welcome aboard," the man said.

I followed the queue of people down the metal corridor. With each step, my anxiety grew. I hated heights. No, scratch that, I hated the idea of *falling* from heights. And there's nothing quite like imagining yourself falling from heights when you're inside an enormous hunk of metal 30,000 feet in the sky.

I found my seat and stowed my luggage. There were three seats in my row. The window seat was taken by an older woman wearing so much jewellery she twinkled and chimed with every movement. I sat in the middle seat beside her.

I stuck in my earbuds and blasted my music. It drowned out the sound of the pilot speaking. It drowned out the sound of the safety video. It drowned out what to do in the event of a water landing.

I didn't want to think about a water landing.

I wanted to think about Grandma. And my friend Olive. And spending the summer at the beach

collecting shells and swimming. The plane taxied down the runway and began its powerful climb into the sky. My stomach dropped, my hands and neck began to sweat. I gripped the armrests tight and pictured my destination.

And it helped. Sort of.

When the plane levelled off, I peeled my hands from the armrests. The woman beside me had the window shade up. A brilliant blue sky speckled with clouds filled the window.

There was a tap on my shoulder. I leaped up, startling the flight attendant who was trying to get my attention.

I plucked out my earbuds.

"Would you like something to drink?" the flight attendant asked.

"Oh," I said. "Um, no. I'm OK."

The flight attendant's drinks' cart rattled as she moved on down the aisle. I started to put my earbuds back in when the walking jewellery advertisement spoke. "Not a fan of flying, eh?" she asked.

"Nope," I said.

The aeroplane suddenly shook and dipped. My heart followed suit. I gasped and grabbed the woman's bracelet-heavy arm.

"It's OK, dear," the woman said reassuringly. "Very few planes actually crash because of turbulence."

I exhaled slowly and tried to calm my nerves. "Thanks," I said.

"No problem." The woman smiled. "Statistically, take-offs and landings are far more dangerous. That's when we're likely to crash."

Just like that, the anxiety was back.

With every shake, every rumble, every dip and turn, my heartbeat sped up and my fingers dug into the armrests harder.

They didn't relax until the wheels touched the tarmac in Bangor.

2

Olive was excited to see me when I reached baggage claim. She rushed straight up to me and hugged me. Olive lived next door to Grandma. We'd been friends since we were both wearing armbands on the beach, but as Olive lived here year-round and I didn't, we only saw each other in the summer. Olive had thick-rimmed glasses. Her shoulder-length hair was dusty blonde this summer.

"So how was your flight?" Olive asked.

"It was fine," I lied.

"My word, Simone," Grandma said. "You are a bean sprout shooting to the sky. You're just like your father." Grandma wrapped me in a comforting hug. She was short. At thirteen, I was just as tall as her. She wore her black hair pulled back in a ponytail.

"Love you, Grandma," I said.

Olive took my hand and led the way back to Grandma's car, a baby-blue classic Volkswagen Beetle. A speckle of rust rimmed each wheel. Otherwise the car was in great shape. She'd bought it after Grandpa died, about three years ago.

"Do you think those long legs will fit in my car?" Grandma asked, nudging me in the side and chuckling at her own joke.

When I climbed into the passenger seat I had to slide the seat back so my knees wouldn't touch the dashboard. I didn't say anything to Grandma about it, but I caught her looking over and smirking as we drove away from the airport.

The city was soon replaced by tall evergreens and a winding two-lane highway. It was amazing how quickly we travelled from the hum of activity to the peacefulness of the country.

As we went, Olive leaned forward between our seats and talked about school being finished for the summer. About her dog Charlie. About the friends at her new school. About pretty much everything that popped into her head.

Soon we were driving along the stretch of oceanside road that led into Sunset Cove. On our right, the deep blue of the Atlantic Ocean met the horizon. I wound my window down. The cool ocean air, with its perfect salty smell, swirled around me and made my hair dance.

I loved that smell. I closed my eyes and breathed it in.

"There's the promenade!" Olive's shout broke my inner calm. "We're meeting my friends there later!"

I peeled one eye open. I had run across that promenade countless times. We had built sandcastles in its shadow for years. But something about the way Olive talked about it made me want to look.

What I saw made my breath catch in my throat.

Looming above the treeline was a gigantic, colourful Ferris Wheel. Its carriages – red, blue, yellow and green – were not moving, but seemed to sway nonetheless.

"Whoa," I whispered.

"Cool, huh?" Olive said. "The carnival has just arrived in town. In the middle of the night! I had no idea it was going to take over the promenade."

As Grandma drove past the promenade, I saw there was a break in the trees.

I spotted more attractions, including a metal rollercoaster and a row of tents with games in them.

Next to the road, three men were hanging a banner on a broken billboard. Two stood on ladders while the other supervised from the ground. The banner read: Forever Fun Carnival.

As we drove past, the man on the ground turned. He wore dusty overalls and a bright red baseball cap pulled low on his head. His hard-edged face was lined with deep creases. He peered at the car. Peered at me.

His gaze made the hair on the back of my neck stand up. Suddenly, I was very cold. I wound up my window.

"Everything OK?" Grandma asked.

I looked in the rear-view mirror. The man was still watching us. He stared at the car until we rounded a corner and he disappeared.

"Yeah," I said. "Just . . . cold, I think."

3

Grandma's house was a one-storey cabin with a huge screened-in porch. It sat at the top of a small hill in a cluster of other cabins, including the one owned by Olive's family. The hill led to a wide beach, where waves lapped at the sand and stones.

As the three of us got out of the car, a large, fluffy white dog raced out to greet us. It barked and jumped and wagged its tail.

"Hey-ya, Charlie," I said, scratching the dog behind an ear. "Miss me, boy?"

As if in response, Charlie barked and licked my hand.

"Come on," Olive said to her dog. "Let's give Simone some time to settle in." Then she and Charlie raced off towards their house.

The inside of Grandma's cabin was cluttered. She had knick-knacks and trinkets everywhere, much of it traced back to her Korean heritage.

I dropped my things in the back bedroom. It was narrow, with a single bed. On the chest of drawers was a mirror covered in photos of me and my grandparents.

Grandma whipped up a meal of rice and fish, and we ate on the porch. I couldn't believe I got to spend the whole summer enjoying freshly cooked meals, with the ocean accompanying our every bite.

"Be safe tonight," Grandma said as she cleared our plates and I grabbed my bike helmet off a hook on the wall.

"We always are," I replied, hurrying out of the door.

Olive was waiting. We hopped on our bikes and cycled down a path through the trees we'd created years ago. The sun cast long shadows and left pockets of light in the forest. It would be dark soon, and we'd have to be more cautious on our way home.

I pedalled hard, sailing off bumps in the path. Low-hanging branches whisked against our shoulders and helmets.

We broke from the last cluster of trees and into the light. The promenade lay straight ahead. Even though it wasn't yet dark, the carnival's lights glowed bright. The Ferris wheel slowly turned, its open carriages filled with laughing kids and adults. Seeing it again made my stomach turn.

Olive must have seen the fear in my eyes. She skidded to a stop. "This'll be fun," she said. "I promise."

The moment I stepped onto the promenade's thick wooden planks, I could feel the rumbling rollercoaster beneath my feet. Olive peered through the crowd.

"I can't see them," she said. Then she clasped a hand around my wrist. "But I can see something that you'll love!"

Tucked away, almost hidden from sight, was an old, glass fortune-teller machine. A statue of a man with a thin, twirling moustache smiled at us. In front of him was a glowing crystal ball. "Let ZOLTAR tell your FUTURE!" was painted on a nearby sign.

Olive dug out some coins. "Here," she said. "You go first."

As silly as these machines were, I did get a kick out of them. So I plucked a coin from Olive's palm and dropped it into the Zoltar machine.

Zoltar's crystal ball began to flicker. The statue's head twisted back and forth. A tinny voice filtered out of the speaker. "Greetings," it said in a thick, unknown accent. "Zoltar knows all. Zoltar sees all. Let the light of my crystal ball guide you on your path."

A whizz and a click, and the flickering stopped. A slip of paper appeared in the slot beside the speaker. I tore it off and read it.

You are right to be scared.

"Is this some kind of joke?" I asked no one in

particular. Or maybe Zoltar. I didn't know. The fortune in my hand was making it tremble. Like plane turbulence. Or a Ferris wheel in the sky.

"Oh, don't take it so seriously," Olive said "My turn!" She inserted another coin and clapped as Zoltar made his speech, then she ripped off her own fortune. I hoped my fears would go away when she read something strange like the silly fortune I'd just received.

"Watch over your friend," Olive read. "She will need your help."

"What?" I grabbed her wrist and pulled the fortune towards me so I could read it for myself.

Olive brushed me off. "Don't worry," she said with a chuckle. "This fortune is total nonsense. I always look out for you."

"Olive!" came a loud voice from the crowd.

A group of kids was walking towards us. The girl in the lead waved to get our attention.

"Guys!" Olive dashed off in their direction. I gave the grinning, maniacal Zoltar one last glare and shoved my stupid fortune into my pocket.

4

Olive introduced me to her friends. There was Gwenda. She had curly brown hair that was this weird combination of perfect and "just out of bed". There were the twins, Steph and Keenan. Steph had long blonde hair, and Keenan had really short hair.

Then there was C.J. She stood out, both in her mannerisms and the fact that she actually stood away from the rest of us. C.J. had a fake-looking smile and flawless dark brown skin.

"Simone is spending the summer at her grandma's," Olive explained. "She just flew in

a couple of hours ago."

"Hi guys," I said with a wave.

"Hi," Keenan and Steph said together. Gwenda waved.

C.J. said nothing, but offered a half-smile. Then she looked off along the promenade. "I'm bored. And I've got my eye on the hoopla stall."

Without another word, she headed along the promenade, expecting the rest of us to just follow along. And we did.

"What's with her?" I asked Olive as we followed closely behind the group.

"She's nice once you get to know her," Olive said.

"Somehow I doubt that," I muttered.

I was frustrated that my time with Olive had become time with Olive and her friends.

We walked along and C.J. bought a whole load of tickets for the carnival. She spent way too many of them throwing beanbags at milk cartons and throwing hoops at old drinks bottles while the others just watched and cheered her on. When she finally did get a hoop on a bottle and the carnival worker tried to give her a purple toy monkey as a prize, she wrinkled her nose and said, "Ugh. No thanks."

Keenan snatched it up and tucked it under one arm. "Purple Monkey, you are mine," he said.

We wandered over to the food stalls, where I bought mini-doughnuts in a tiny paper bag. They were heavenly. Then Olive and I went on the waltzers. We laughed as the ride spun, pressing us against each other. With each twirl, the carnival became a blur of lights and motion.

"That was amazing!" Olive and I cheered as the ride came to a stop.

Less amazing was the feeling I got as I stepped back onto the promenade. The wood beneath me felt like it was still moving, and I regretted the way I'd inhaled my mini-doughnuts.

"I need to sit down," I said, staggering towards a nearby bench.

I sat, head bowed, while my stomach calmed.

Olive flopped down next to me and handed me a bottle of water. "Are you all right?" she asked.

"Yeah," I said. "Apparently flying across the country, eating a bag of mini-doughnuts and violently spinning in circles is bad for the stomach. Who knew?"

I gave myself another moment, then breathed deep through my nose and stood.

"OK," I said. "What's next?"

"I want to go on another ride," Gwenda suggested. "Maybe . . . the rollercoaster?"

"Ooooh." Steph nodded. "Good idea."

"Agreed," Keenan said.

The last thing me and my upset stomach needed was to get on the rollercoaster. I shook my head. "I'll sit this one out," I said.

"Come on, Summer Girl," C.J. said with a coy smile. "It'll be fun. Right, Olive?"

Olive looked at me, then over at C.J., then back, as if she was watching a tennis match. "I mean—" she started.

C.J. didn't let her finish. "I knew it!" she said, sliding her arm into Olive's and locking them together. "Olive's on board!" She began to strut away, my best friend in tow, leaving me behind.

And so, as I'd been doing all night, I followed them towards the rickety rollercoaster.

5

As we neared the rollercoaster, I heard my dad's voice in my head, quoting one of his favourite films. "I've got a bad feeling about this . . ." I did have a bad feeling I couldn't shake, and it wasn't just the mini-doughnuts.

The rollercoaster wasn't very tall, certainly not like the ones in amusement parks and definitely not as tall as the Ferris wheel. But what it lacked in height it made up for in twists and turns.

As I looked around, it seemed as if the carnival crowd was thinning out. When we'd arrived, there had been people packed along the promenade.

Even though it wasn't terribly late yet and the carnival wasn't due to close for a few more hours, it seemed less crowded now.

"Gwenda, you're up front with me!" C.J. chirped. She let go of Olive's arm and hurried over to snatch up Gwenda. Olive looked confused. Steph and Keenan were sure to pair off together, so that left Olive and me as a twosome. And if I wasn't going, then Olive would be in a carriage on her own. C.J. was a lot cleverer – and more conniving – than I'd first given her credit for.

"I suppose you need someone to sit with," I said quietly to Olive.

"It's OK," she said. "I know you don't like heights."

"Or she's just trying to get attention," I heard C.J. mutter under her breath.

"No," I said, suddenly drawn by the urge to prove C.J. wrong. "I'll go with you."

I tried not to pay attention to the ride as we stood in the queue. I tried to ignore the groaning metal framework, and how the promenade shuddered every time a train of rollercoaster carriages passed. I tried not to imagine the ride crumpling or toppling over.

A ticket collector stood at the front of the queue. He reminded me of the man I'd seen earlier in the day. He had the same deep, chiselled creases etched across his face. He held out a hand and wiggled his bony fingers at me. "Ticket, please," he said with a grin.

The man's dark, empty eyes and too-wide smile were creeping me out so much I almost turned back. Almost.

"Front car!" C.J. shouted. She and Gwenda climbed in.

Each car in the train held four people, two rows of two. Steph and Keenan also wanted the front car, so they climbed into a different one. This meant Olive and I were in the back, behind C.J. and Gwenda. Fine by me. I slid into the old metal seat, trying to hide how much my hands were shaking.

Olive lowered the bar across our laps until it clicked into place. It felt tight against me. I gripped

the bar hard and made sure it was secure.

"Are you sure you're OK?" Olive whispered.

"Never better," I said through chattering teeth. I sneaked a glance over my shoulder at the carriages behind us.

The other trains, six of them, sat empty. We were the only ones on the ride. I was certain there had been people queuing behind us. Hadn't there?

"Wait . . ." I started. " Where is . . . ?"

The carriage jerked forward before I could finish. I spun my head back around. C.J. had her arms up. The carriage slowly rounded a corner, then lurched forward as we began to climb.

I felt every click of the chain beneath us as the carriage rose. To my left, the ocean was inky black as far as the eye could see. The moon had retreated into the clouds, making the carnival the only beacon of light.

We kept climbing. I squeezed my eyes shut and held onto the bar even tighter.

It felt like an eternity. The clicking.

The climbing. "How are we not at the top yet?"
I whispered. The wind caught my words and
swallowed them.

The coaster swayed back and forth. The metal
track and support beams shuddered and moaned
like an injured beast.

"Here we go!" C.J. screeched.

The climbing slowed, slowed . . . slowed.

The carriage surged forward.

And we plummeted!

6

I screamed, but the wind slammed against my face and drowned the sound out. The sudden drop made my stomach claw its way into my throat and lodge itself there.

We hit the bottom of the track and twisted hard left. Olive and her friends cheered and hooted. With each turn, it felt like the car could topple off the track.

We rose and fell, rattled and clattered. Excitement cut through the fear, and for the briefest of moments, a smile flickered across my face. It was gone in an instant as the carriage's brakes engaged with a squeal and we slid back to the platform.

I'd done it. I'd survived the rollercoaster.

I staggered out of the car on wobbly legs. The platform felt like it was swaying, as if I was on the deck of a ship.

"That was so much fun!" C.J. said, practically skipping down the platform and back onto the promenade with Gwenda. Keenan proudly held up the stuffed toy and proclaimed, "Purple Monkey gives it two opposable thumbs up!"

"Wait up!" Olive brushed past me to catch up with them.

Behind me, the rollercoaster clattered as another set of passengers began to climb the first rise. As I looked more closely, though, I noticed there weren't any people. The carriages were empty. It reached the top, shot down, loudly clattered past me and curved away. The structure shuddered as they vanished.

Tink . . . tink . . . tink . . .

Something fell from above, hitting the coaster's metal support beams and landing on the promenade. It was hard to see through the thick shadows under the coaster.

But I saw it. And when I realized what it was, my stomach sank as if it was back on the rollercoaster.

Had a piece of the rollercoaster really just fallen off? And was I the only person who saw it?

A small plastic fence had been set up around the ride for safety, but I wanted to confirm my suspicions. So I stepped closer.

It was a shiny metal screw.

The shadows under the rollercoaster moved, startling me. A figure emerged, a man in dirty overalls and a baseball cap.

The man from the highway.

Without a word, he bent down, picked up the fallen screw, and pocketed it. I tried to retreat, but my feet wouldn't move. The man locked eyes with me. The shivers that had coursed through me the first time I'd seen him returned stronger than before.

He vanished back into the shadows.

I was finished with this place. I wanted to go back to Grandma's.

"Olive!?" I shouted as I stumbled away from the rollercoaster. I ran along the promenade, looking for my friend. "Olive!"

"Simone?!" Olive cried back. She and the others had stopped up ahead. Maybe to wait for me, but probably not. C.J. stood with her arms crossed while the others threw Purple Monkey around. None of them seemed to notice that the crowd was basically gone now.

"What's up?" Olive asked as I reached her.

"I'm leaving," I said.

"What?"

"I'm going back to Grandma's," I said. "This place . . ." It felt weird to say it out loud. "This place has been creeping me out since the moment we got here."

Olive spoke in a low voice. "Is this about my friends?" She cast a glance over her shoulder.

"What?" I replied. "No."

"Then stay," Olive said. "You liked the rollercoaster, didn't you?"

Until a piece of it fell off! I thought.

"I just . . . wanna go home," I said. "I want to hang out on the beach. And read books. And swim. And collect shells and rocks. With you."

"So it *is* about my friends." Olive put her hands on her hips and glared at me.

I shook my head and said, "Whatever." Then I stalked away.

"Bye, Summer Girl!" C.J. sang.

I didn't turn around. I walked through the carnival, now practically empty, until I reached the exit.

A twinkle of light caught the corner of my eye. I turned to see Zoltar smiling at me. Angrily, I stomped over to the machine and dug in my pocket. I still had some money left.

I don't know why I wanted another fortune. Maybe to prove the stupid thing was random, that it had a whole load of different sayings in it and that my first fortune was a fluke.

I dropped a coin into the slot and let Zoltar glow and flicker and talk in its cheesy voice.

I wasn't amused. All I wanted was the slip of paper at the end.

When it came, I ripped it off and immediately read it. "You are right to be scared," I whispered.

I'd got exactly the same fortune as before.

7

"Arrgh!" I ripped up the fortune, dropped it on the promenade, and stomped on it for good measure. Zoltar smiled back at me, a glint of menace in his painted eyes.

"What is going on with this place?" I didn't say it loud, but my voice seemed to carry. I glanced around the promenade, but there weren't any families around. No couples holding hands and carrying oversized stuffed toys like Purple Monkey. Nobody but me.

Where had everyone gone?

"Hello?" I called out.

No one answered. But there was movement ahead. A man appeared from behind one of the tents, shuffling out to the middle of the promenade. Another carnival worker.

And he looked just like the man in the overalls.

I quickly ran off the promenade and towards the path where Olive and I had left our bikes. Sand from the beach kicked up behind me. It slipped inside my shoes, grinding between my toes. I didn't care.

It wasn't until I reached the bikes, propped against a tree at the edge of the wooded path, that I noticed how very dark it was. The moon was still hidden in the clouds, snuffing out its usual blue glow. It was as if the carnival was sapping the light out of everything around it.

I grabbed the handlebars and turned my bike towards the path in the woods. At least, where I thought the path in the woods was. All I could see was blackness.

And it was quiet. So very quiet.

When I noticed the absolute silence around me,

I couldn't stop shivering. The carnival was not far away. I should've still been able to hear its creepy music or hear the clattering rollercoaster. But there was nothing. Not even the ocean waves made noise.

The black woods loomed before me.

Quiet.

Empty.

There was no way I could ride back to Grandma's house in the dark by myself.

So I did what I should have done straight away. I dug out my phone and called Grandma for a lift.

She picked up on the third ring. "Hi, sweetheart. Is everything OK?" she asked. It sounded as if I'd woken her up. "Are you having a good time with Olive and her friends?"

"No, Grandma," I said. "I need a lift home." I had begun to cry, and used the bottom of my T-shirt to wipe my eyes and nose.

There was a crackle on the phone. A long pause.

Then: "Simone?"

Grandma sounded confused. "Simone, are you

there, honey?"

"Grandma?" I said, louder. "Grandma. Yes. It's me. I'm here. I want to come home." My voice shook.

Another long pause. More crackling.

"Well, this silly thing just isn't working," Grandma said, more to herself than to me. "Simone, if that's you, I can't hear a thing. Try calling me—"

Crackle. And then she was gone.

The town of Sunset Cove wasn't exactly in the middle of nowhere. Reception and dropped calls shouldn't have been a problem. Frustrated, I began to dial Grandma's number again.

As I punched 'Send,' my phone blanked out.

Black screen.

Dead.

8

"What?" I punched at the phone screen and pressed the power button. It had to be a mistake. I should have had enough charge to make it through the night.

But then I thought about the plane journey. I'd blasted music for two-plus hours in an attempt not to think about crashing. Maybe my phone's battery was sapped.

I looked around at the darkness and thought about riding my bike back alone. *This would be so much better with Olive,* I thought.

Maybe I could convince Olive to come back

with me. Or at least convince her to let me use her phone to call Grandma. Grandma was probably worried that I hadn't immediately called back.

So I strode back into the Forever Fun Carnival, past the Zoltar machine, and towards the rollercoaster. The promenade was nearly empty now. The only sounds came from the clattering of empty rides and the tinkling, eerie music.

Olive and her friends weren't hard to spot. They were walking together down the middle of the promenade.

C.J. was, of course, the first one to see me. "She's back!" She threw her arms up as if she wanted to hug me. "What a fun surprise, Summer Girl."

"Stop calling me that," I said. I turned to Olive. "Can I use your phone? I need to call Grandma and my phone is dead."

"Grandma?" Gwenda repeated with a snigger. Great, even the rest of Olive's crew was starting to make fun of me.

Olive took my arm and pulled me aside. "Simone, you're pale and sweating," she said.

"What's going on?"

"Don't you see?" I tried to whisper, to keep myself calm. But it was hard. The words pushed their way out, louder than I'd intended. "This carnival . . . it's weird. The people working here all look the same. The rides are falling apart. This whole place is deserted and you don't even seem to notice."

Olive's face scrunched up in confusion. "What are you talking about?"

"We're the only ones here," I said.

"No," Olive said, shaking her head and sliding an arm around my shoulder. "We're not."

"Wait . . . what?" I looked around.

Olive was right. The crowd hadn't disappeared at all. There were people everywhere. I turned in a full circle, taking in the carnival with awed disbelief. "But–" I started. "Just a second ago . . ."

"Look," Olive said calmly, "you've had a long day. I get it. You're tired and jet-lagged and maybe those mini-doughnuts really disagreed with you. But there's nothing unusual about this place.

Nothing to be scared of."

I pulled the fortune out of my pocket. "What about this, though?" I asked. "'You're right to be scared.'"

Olive did the same – took her fortune out and held it next to mine. "'Watch over your friend,'" she said. "So here I am. Watching over you. OK?"

I took a deep breath and looked out again at the people of Sunset Cove enjoying the carnival. I heard screams of delight from the rollercoaster and waltzers. The delicious scent of hot dogs drifted through the sea breeze. Kids were walking everywhere, holding ice cream cones that dripped down to their hands.

I crumpled up Zoltar's fortune and dropped it onto the promenade. It slipped between a thin gap in two planks of wood and vanished from sight. A wave of relief washed over me.

I was fine.

"One more ride and we'll head back home together," Olive said. "Promise."

"Hey, you two!" C.J. called out. She and the

others were watching us. "We're heading to the Ferris wheel. Are you coming or what?"

I looked over at Olive, whose arm was still draped over my shoulder.

"Sure," I blurted out before I could stop myself.

9

My fear of the Forever Fun Carnival had subsided. But I was still deathly afraid of heights. So why I'd agreed to join the group on the Ferris wheel made little sense. Maybe it was Olive's confidence and support. Or maybe it was because I'd already bested the rollercoaster.

Whatever it was, here we stood, in the queue for the Ferris wheel. Just a normal group of kids (and one stuffed purple monkey), enjoying a night at the carnival.

"How are you now?" Olive whispered as we neared the front of the queue. The young man taking tickets looked nothing like the creepy old man from the highway. Only his red baseball cap was the same.

"Great," I answered. And it was mostly the truth.

The carriage waiting at the bottom of the Ferris wheel was purple. Keenan insisted it was a sign he and Steph should go first.

"Tickets, please," the man said to Steph and Keenan. They each put a pair of red tickets in his hand and took their places.

"See you on the other side," Steph said. Keenan waved Purple Monkey's hand and they began to climb towards the night sky.

C.J. and Gwenda went next, handing over tickets and climbing into a yellow carriage.

I had two tickets in my hand. Nervously, I passed them to the man. "Climb aboard," he said with a smile. A red car had slowed to a stop at the bottom. I got in and waited for Olive.

But Olive was still talking to the ticket man. She searched her pockets, concerned. "I know I had

more than one," I heard her say.

"You need two tickets to ride," the man replied.

The bar above slammed down, startling me. "Olive?!" I shouted.

Olive looked up at me. "What's going on?" she asked.

The ticket man smiled wide. Creases formed across his face, and he suddenly didn't look as young. "The ride must go on," he said to me. "Your friend will catch the next carriage."

My heart thundered against my ribcage. I tried to pull the bar up, to get out of the carriage and back to Olive. It was too late, though.

With a long creak, the Ferris wheel began to move again. I lifted off the ground, away from the promenade, away from Olive.

"Simone!" Olive cried.

"Olive!" I shouted back. I bent over and tried to look down and find her. All I could see, though, was the carnival getting smaller and smaller as I kept rising.

"What's going on down there, Summer Girl?" C.J. asked from above. She and Gwenda laughed. Their carriage creaked back and forth over my head, as if they were rocking it. Higher, out of my sight, Keenan made monkey noises while his sister cheered him on.

I held on tight to the bar. My knuckles were bone-white. The Ferris wheel did not stop for more people. I crept higher and higher. In each direction, the blackened waves of the Atlantic Ocean were all I could see.

Cold sweat ran down my forehead and into my eyes, making them sting.

So I squeezed them shut.

"Just make it one time around," I whispered to myself. "Get back to the bottom and Olive will be there waiting for you."

Time stretched as I kept rising. I couldn't hear C.J. and Gwenda laughing any more. I couldn't hear their carriage swinging. Keenan's monkey howls were gone as well. It was just me and the groaning, straining sound of the Ferris wheel.

Even with my eyes closed, I knew when I'd reached the top. Instead of rising, my car began moving backwards. In just a second, I'd start my descent towards the promenade again and this tortuous ride would be over.

That was when the Ferris wheel shuddered to a stop.

10

I hung suspended in the air, high above the
promenade. I was too terrified to look down. The
wind sneaked up on me. It howled and made my
hair dance. I could feel each beat of my heart in my
ears. Each breath was a thin rasp.

Forever. I was going to be here . . . forever.

Alone.

I don't know how long I sat swaying, eyes
closed, praying I'd see Grandma and Olive and my
parents again. But then the ride trembled and my
carriage began to move again.

"Oh, thank goodness," I whispered. I peeled one hand from the bar and used it to wipe the tears from my eyes. I was getting lower and lower. And the closer I got to the ground, the safer I felt.

I'd made it.

"Olive?" I shouted when I'd nearly reached the bottom. "I'm here! And I wanna get off this stupid thing!"

When I'd made it down, when I could see the promenade beneath me, I tried to lift the bar. "Let me off!" I said to the young man operating the ride.

Only he wasn't there any more. Standing at the base of the Ferris wheel was the old man from the highway. Red baseball cap. Overalls. Wide smile that looked eerily like Zoltar's.

"What?" The panic was back. "No," I whispered, looking beyond the man, at the promenade. "NOOO!!"

The carnival was gone. No rides. No food stalls. No crowds of people. No C.J. or Gwenda or Keenan or Steph.

And no Olive.

I was alone. It was just me and the creepy old man and the Ferris wheel.

From the shadows, more figures emerged. More carnival workers. And they all looked the same, wearing the same crazed smile as the old man. Identical creased faces and red caps and overalls.

They all stared at me.

"Let me off!" I shouted again. I tried harder to free myself from the Ferris wheel. But the carriage didn't stop. Soon I was climbing towards the sky again.

I looked at the carriages around me. They were all empty. The group of carnival workers, with their identical faces and expressions, craned their necks to watch as I rose into the black night again.

Something fluttered through the air in front of me. It struck me on the chest, then fell to my lap. I let go of the bar with one hand and grabbed it.

It was a slip of paper. A fortune. My fortune. Only now, the words had changed.

WE WARNED YOU, it read.

"Help!" I shouted at the top of my lungs as I climbed higher . . . higher . . .

Higher.

GLOSSARY

conniving scheming or plotting something in secret

eerie strange and frightening

etched deeply marked

glint sparkle or flash

heritage traditions and beliefs that a country or society considers an important part of its history

identical exactly the same

loom appear suddenly or in a scary manner

lurch move in a sudden and uneven way

mannerism certain behaviour showing how someone acts

plummet drop sharply

reception quality of a mobile phone signal in a particular area

speckle tiny piece, spot or mark

tortuous painful or upsetting

trinket small, cheap object

turbulence swirling winds that create strong air resistance; turbulence can quickly slow down an aircraft

FACE YOUR FEAR!

Now that you've read the story, it's no longer only inside this book. It's also in your brain. Can your brain help you answer the prompts below?

1. Simone isn't happy about spending time with Olive's friends. Why do you think Simone is hurt by having to spend time with Olive's new friends?

2. Simone describes all the carnival workers as having identical faces. Why do you think that is?

3. Olive was told by the fortune-teller machine to watch over Simone. Write about what you would do if a fortune-teller machine told you to watch over your best friend.

4. Simone feels worried about her flight from Chicago to Maine. Write down all the things Simone experiences on her plane trip that make her feel anxious.

5. Just before Simone gets onto the Ferris wheel, Olive discovers she can't get on. Write down what you think would have happened if Olive had got on the ride. Would the story have ended the same way?

The Lost Lenore

The Gulliver Giant

The Minotaur Maze

The Final Frankenstein

only from Raintree